BALI RAI

THE HARDER THEY FALL

Barrington Stoke

First published in 2017 in Great Britain by
Barrington Stoke Ltd
18 Walker Street, Edinburgh, EH3 7LP

www.barringtonstoke.co.uk

Text © 2017 Bali Rai

The moral right of Bali Rai to be identified as the author
of this work has been asserted in accordance with the
Copyright, Designs and Patents Act, 1988

A CIP catalogue record for this book is available
from the British Library upon request

ISBN: 978-1-78112-682-0

Printed in China by Leo

CONTENTS

Batman Begins

I always wanted to write my own story. I always wanted to be the hero. A proper human hero, not someone with super powers.

In my story, I'd have a friend who was in danger and I'd have to save them. There would be a girl, too. A cute, funny girl, who liked all the things I liked. We'd save the day and fall in love and ...

Thing is, I didn't have any friends in the real world. Just Mum and Dad, and they don't count, do they? The girl was just a dream, too.

And then things got weird. There *was* a friend, there *was* a girl, and there *was* a story to tell. The story could have been called "The Calloway Files" or "Calloway Returns" or something like that. That's me – Calloway. The story could have been a comic or a graphic novel. But in the end, it wasn't about me.

In the end it was all about Jacob.

1

Reign of Terror

Anu Patel twisted my ear lobe. Her fingers were skinny and her nails were bright orange. When she wasn't snarling, she was kind of pretty. Only right now she *was* snarling.

"*Why* haven't you done it?" she demanded. "I've got customers, you goggle-faced geek."

"I didn't have time," I said. "I had a yoga class."

"*Yoga?*" she said. "What are you, Cal – a hippy?"

I did homework for Anu, and she sold it to other pupils. She called it her business. I was her only employee.

"Please," I said. "My ear hurts ..."

"News flash, dork!" she said. "It's *supposed* to hurt."

I tried to pull away but that made the pain worse. I decided to try a new tactic.

"Violence never solves anything," I told her.

"Oh *please!*" Anu said. "Keep that peace and love rubbish for your yoga class."

At last she let go.

"Get it done this lunchtime," she warned. "Or I'll pull your ear off!"

As she marched away, I could smell sweet perfume and hear the *clack* of expensive shoes. We didn't have a school uniform and Anu Patel was rich. Even her P.E. kit was designer. Oh, and she was a bully, but I guess you got that.

*

Later, Mrs Collier the librarian had a word with me. "Are you getting trouble from Anu Patel?" she asked.

"No, Miss," I said.

"Are you sure, Calloway?" she said. "A Year 7 said she'd hurt you."

"She was just messing about," I said.

Mrs Collier didn't look convinced but she let me go anyway. I grabbed my bag and headed to my form room. When I arrived, a big freckly lad with short ginger hair was standing at the front next to the teacher.

"Newbie!" someone shouted.

The new boy glared at us all.

"This is Jacob," Mr Gossage said. "He's joining Year 9."

Jacob went a bit red.

"*Ahh!*" Freya said. "Look – he's gone all shy!"

Some lads sniggered, but Freya hadn't been teasing. I'd known her since nursery and she wasn't ever mean to anyone.

"Freya, Cal – could you show Jacob around next lesson?" Mr Gossage asked.

"Er, suppose so," I said, and Freya smiled.

Freya led Jacob and me around school, starting with Maths and Science. Jacob had stopped scowling, but now he just looked bored.

"Any questions?" Freya asked.

I tried to make eye contact with her, but I couldn't. Freya was my secret crush – Selina Kyle to my Batman. She had dark hair and a button nose. Her eyes were big and brown, and her skin was pale. She wore glasses like me, only hers had cool frames. She was cute.

"Jacob?" she asked again. "Questions?"

"Nah," Jacob said. "All looks the same to me, innit?"

"Fab!" Freya said. "Let's go to Art – my favourite!"

Freya didn't notice how bored Jacob was – she was all smiles and excitement. I was happy to be with her, and curious about Jacob too.

He only spoke to say he was bored. His clothes looked shabby – his shirt was almost grey, not white. I noticed that his shoes were all scuffed.

"We done?" he asked, when we returned to the front door.

"Yep!" Freya said. "Now, I'll take you to your next lesson. What is it?"

"Dunno," Jacob said, and he stared at his timetable.

"Shall I look?" I offered.

"What?" Jacob snapped. "You think I can't read or summat, bruv?"

"I was just offering to help," I said to my feet.

"Stuff your help!" Jacob said. "I'm off ..."

And with that he trudged away.

"Not exactly friendly, is he?" Freya said. "Never mind. We've got English next, haven't we?"

I nodded. Freya had said "we" like there *was* a "*we*".

"Calloway?" she asked.

"Hmm?"

"Why are you grinning?"

"Oh, no reason." I hadn't even realised I was.

At the end of the corridor, we saw Jacob kick a door open so hard it slammed into the wall.

2

Justice League

Mum was making veggie shepherd's pie when I got home.

"Help me mash these potatoes, will you?" she asked. "How was school?"

I thought of how Anu had twisted my ear until it throbbed.

"Great," I lied. "A new boy started today. Me and Freya showed him around."

"Freya Saunders?" Mum asked. "She's a lovely girl – you've been friends since nursery."

I scowled. Why was Mum doing that weird parent thing of telling me stuff that I already knew?

"Pretty, too," Mum added, as she took carrots and broccoli from the fridge.

"Mum!" I groaned. I felt myself blush.

Mum grinned and nodded at the table.

"Plates, Cal ..."

*

When everything was ready, Dad strolled in from the garden. He'd converted the shed into a studio for his work. Today he was in a lab coat covered in paint, and his blond hair was all crazy scientist. Sticky tape held his glasses together.

"Hey Cal!" he said. "You didn't say you were back."

"You were in the shed," I pointed out.

"The *studio*, Cal," he said. "I've been painting."

"You painted yourself, by the look of you," Mum joked.

Dad stuck out his tongue and Mum laughed.

"Let's eat," she said.

As I wolfed down the pie, my parents talked about boring adult stuff. And then Mum cleared her throat.

"I've been thinking," she said.

Mum had crazy ideas all the time. My yoga classes were one. Last year, we became vegans for a while, after Mum read a book called *The Truth About Milk*. I pushed a piece of broccoli around my plate, as I waited for her latest brainwave.

"I want to volunteer at a food bank," she said.

I frowned. "What's a food bank?" I asked.

"It's a charity place that gives free food to people in need," she said. "I think we should all volunteer. I was thinking three times a week. We could even help on Christmas Day."

"You can't *make* Cal help," Dad said. "He has to decide for himself."

I shrugged.

"I don't mind helping," I said. "But not on Christmas Day."

"OK." Mum smiled at me. "I'll find out when they need us."

Dad groaned again and Mum gave him a stern look.

"We need to rebalance our spirits," she said. "As a family."

Dad went off to read a book, Mum went upstairs to meditate, and I was alone. It was my turn to clear up and wash the dishes. Then I went to my room to do my homework.

*

Later, Dad came to ask if I was OK.

"Yeah," I said. "It's just ..."

"Just what, kid?"

"Like, are we evil because we have enough money when other people don't?" I asked.

"No!" Dad said. "Of course not. Life isn't easy, Cal, and sometimes bad things happen that bring people down."

"But what if every rich person gave money to poor people?" I asked. "Wouldn't that help?"

"Yes," Dad said. "But not everyone thinks like we do." He sat down next to me. I could tell he'd just smoked his one night-time roll-up.

"You know what, Calloway Gill-Smith?" he said with his stinky cigarette breath.

"What?"

"I'm happy that we think alike, but we don't have to. I love you anyway." He kissed me on my head and left.

3

Tales of the Demon

A few days later, Anu tripped me up. As I fell, I wondered what would rebalance her spirit.

"You OK, Cal?" Miss Spargo asked, as I picked myself up and sat down.

"No, Miss," Anu said. "He's a dork."

All Anu's mates giggled.

"That's not acceptable, Anu," Miss Spargo said. "Next time you'll go into isolation. Clear?"

Anu looked away. "Over-react much?" she muttered.

*

As soon as Maths was over, I rushed to the library.

I was there a while before I spotted Jacob. He was sitting alone, with a Batman novel. I went over to say hello.

"*Tales of the Demon*," I said. "That's awesome. I love Batman."

He closed the book. "Get lost, geek," he said.

"You should try the others," I told him. "Like *Year One* by Frank Miller."

Jacob shook his head. "I ain't like *you*," he said. "I weren't reading it cos I *want* to."

"You looked like you were," I said. "I saw you."

"Yeah?" he asked. "Well, that makes you a stalker. Bet you fancy me!"

He pushed back in his chair and stood up. "Shove yer effing Batman!" he shouted.

"What's going on?" Mrs Collier asked, as the door slammed in her face.

"Jacob got angry," I said. "I don't know why."

"Don't worry," Mrs Collier told me. "He doesn't seem very happy today, that's all."

I wanted to know why Jacob was sad, but I didn't ask. Instead, I put *Tales of the Demon* back on the shelf.

*

At lunch, I was eating my falafel wrap when the dinner hall erupted with screams and shouts of "*Fight! Fight!*" When I looked up, I saw a Year 10 called Myles Granger and his mates shoving Jacob. Jacob went for Myles, and they punched and kicked him, then pushed him across a table.

"STOP THIS AT ONCE!" I heard Ms Jenkins yell. She was ex-Army and no one messed with her. Then the Head, Mr Ahmed, appeared.

"HOW DARE YOU!" he bellowed, right in Myles's face. "MY OFFICE – NOW!"

Myles trudged out, followed by his mates.

Ms Jenkins had hold of Jacob. I could see him calm down, as he wiped his face on his sleeve and followed her out. As they walked past, I asked Jacob if he was OK.

"Do one, freak!" he snapped.

"Leave him be, Cal," Ms Jenkins said.

I turned back to my lunch, embarrassed.

"Poor Jacob," Freya said, as she sat down next to me. "The way those boys picked on him is horrible ... But that smells nice," she went on, and she took a bite of my wrap. "You don't mind, do you?" she asked, chewing and talking at once. "I'm starving ..."

I felt my cheeks grow hot and my mouth dry.

"Er ... yeah – I mean, *no* ..." I managed.

"Good!" Freya said. "Can I have the rest of it then?"

*

Later, at the end of last lesson, Anu and her friends huddled together to gossip about Jacob.

"How smelly is he?" Anu said.

"I swear those jeans could stand up by themselves!" a girl called Maddie said with a giggle. "You can *see* the dirt on them. Gross!"

"Yeah," said Anu. "Like, Tesco jeans are ten quid. That's not expensive, is it? Even for a chav."

"Don't be so mean," I said.

Anu fixed me with a stare. "Are you talking to *me*?" she asked, and she pointed at her face.

"Yes," I said. I was trying not to shake. "It's really not fair to be rude about Jacob when he isn't here."

Anu sighed and stood up. "Dear, oh dear," she said.

Next thing, Anu shoved me and I fell to the floor. My glasses went flying.

"Oops!" Anu sneered. "The poor geek tripped. Shall I get your mummy for you?"

I didn't reply, and Anu bent down beside me.

"I tell you what to do," she warned. "When I push, nerds like you fall over. It's how life works, Cal. The hardest come first. Understand?"

And, with that, Anu punched me hard in the stomach.

"OWWWW!!!!"

I felt tears in my eyes but I knew I couldn't cry in front of her.

"Don't ever back-chat me again," Anu added.

She slapped my face a couple of times and then at last she left me alone. I heard the door slam as she strode off with her mates, laughing and jeering.

I sat up and tried to clear my head.

"I found these for you," a voice said.

It was Freya. She held out my glasses and I saw that one of the arms had fallen off.

"I've got some tape," she said. "In my bag ..."

"Er, thanks," I said. Somehow I felt a whole lot better.

"You're welcome," Freya said. "Come on, up you get ..."

4

The Outsiders

After that, no one saw Jacob for a week. And when he did reappear, he was really quiet. I wanted to say hello, but I was too scared that he might snap at me again. So I left him alone.

Then, one afternoon, Mum was waiting after school. She was in full-on hippy mode in a yellow hat, a navy anorak, ripped jeans and muddy green wellies. I hoped Anu and her gang didn't spot her.

"Hey, Cal!" Mum gave me a big hug. "How was your day?"

"Good, but why are you here?" I said.

"It's our first day!" she said. "I've got Verity with me."

Verity was our red and white camper van. She was old and rusty and really slow.

"What first day?" I asked.

Mum ruffled my hair. "At the food bank, remember?" she said.

I *had* forgotten. In my bag, I had homework – mine and Anu's.

"But I've got stuff to do," I said.

"No problem," said Mum. "You'll have plenty of time later."

There was no point in protesting. When Mum decided to do something, we did it. We trundled across the city to the hall of St Margaret's Church.

A friendly vicar greeted us as we went in.

"I'm Toby Akinfela," the vicar said. It's good of you to join us." He looked at me and smiled. "And who's this?"

"I'm Cal," I replied. "Calloway Gill-Smith."

Toby smiled again. "Calloway?" he asked. "Like the American jazz man?"

I nodded. Mum and Dad named me after Cab Calloway, a singer who had died before I was born. I had seen loads of pictures of him – he was always smiling and wearing crazy baggy suits with two-tone shoes. We didn't have much in common.

"What an excellent name!" Toby said. "Well, do come in …"

Inside, I counted eight other volunteers. Mum went off to chat to them. I was the only kid.

"Come with me, Cal," Toby said. "I'll show you the ropes – you can give Martin a hand."

He took me over to a big wall of shelves. On the floor were boxes of tins.

"Sort box by box," the guy called Martin told me. "Look, each shelf is split into sections. If you could stack the cans in the right place …"

"No problem," I said, and I put my bag down.

"We don't have many young volunteers," Toby told me. "It's great to see you here."

Over the next hour, I helped sort tins of fruit, vegetables, soup – all sorts. A few dented cans wobbled as I stacked them. Then, I dropped some spaghetti hoops. A woman in a sky blue headscarf helped me to tidy up.

"*Oops!*" she teased.

As I worked, the hall got more and more busy. I looked up to see where Mum was, and that's when I spotted Jacob over by the doors. I stepped back, and prayed he hadn't clocked me. His face was bright red and he looked annoyed.

Then he yelled, "NO, MUM!!!" at the woman next to him – and everyone turned his way.

Toby went over, but Jacob flared up at him too. Then he stormed out.

"Don't worry," Martin said. "That happens sometimes."

"Why?" I asked.

"It's horrible being poor," Martin said and I saw that two of his front teeth were missing. "You start to feel ashamed, son. Like, people reckon you're a scrounger."

"But we're not here to make people feel bad," I said.

"I know," Martin said. "But if you have to ask for help, it can hurt your pride. Make you feel useless."

"You used to be poor?" I asked.

Martin laughed. "Still am, you daft lad," he said. "But least I'm not homeless now."

"Why the long face?" Mum asked a few minutes later as she offered me and Martin a cup of tea. "What's up?"

"The boy who just stormed off," I said. "He's the new lad at school."

"Really?" Mum said. Then she strode over to Jacob's mum.

"Oi, lazybones!" Martin said, and he nudged me with a bony elbow. "Come on, these shelves won't stack themselves."

*

"It's adult stuff," Mum said at home when I asked her what she'd said to Jacob's mum.

"Did you mention me?" I asked. I was worried Jacob would find out.

"Course not," Mum said. "I was just checking she was OK."

So perhaps Jacob didn't know that I'd seen him. I relaxed.

"What's the big deal?" Mum asked.

"He didn't look happy," I said. "Martin said he might be ashamed."

"Why would he be ashamed?" Mum asked.

"I don't know," I told her. "I just don't want to upset him."

Jacob was a loner at school, always in trouble with the teachers and the bullies. Myles Granger and Anu and her gang would make his life hell if they found out about the food bank.

"You could always make friends with him," Mum said.

"What if he doesn't want to be my friend?" I asked.

Mum ruffled my hair. "No harm in trying, is there?" she said.

5

Geek Love Island

The next morning, Jacob and I were both in the library at break. I watched him take *Year One* off the shelf, the Batman book I'd recommended.

I thought about what Mum had said, about how I should make friends with him, and I decided to talk to him about the book.

"One of my all-time favourites," I said. "It's awesome."

Jacob looked up and I saw that he had a dark bruise on his left cheek.

"I ain't reading it because I *like* it," he said. "I *have* to read something."

"But you had a Batman book the other day too – and I've got loads at home," I told him. "Maybe you could come round ..."

Jacob's smirk stopped me in my tracks.

"You what?" he said.

"Like, if you want to be friends," I said.

The smirk turned into a laugh. I felt very stupid.

"Friends?" he said. "Yeah, like I need *you* ..."

And that was the start of a *very* strange day.

*

At lunch, I was walking to the Art department, when someone whispered my name.

It was Freya. For some reason, she was hiding behind some folded tables under the orange stairs that led to Humanities.

"Freya?" I said, confused.

"Hurry!" she said. "Hide!"

She pulled me under the stairs, and I hit my head.

"Oww!"

"Sshh!" she said. "Anu hangs around here at lunch."

We ducked, just as Anu and Maddie came out of the Girls' toilets. They strolled past like they were queens of the school. A little Year 7 boy saw them and turned to run away.

"Oi!" Anu shouted. She grabbed him by his backpack and started to swing him around and push him to and fro with Maddie. Maddie was giggling in a really nasty way.

Then I saw that Freya was filming the whole thing on her phone.

"What are you doing?" I whispered. "That won't help that poor kid."

"Yes it will," she whispered back. "I'm gathering evidence."

Just then Mr Ahmed appeared and Anu and Maddie scuttled off.

"What evidence?" I asked Freya as we came out from under the stairs.

Freya swiped her phone screen and held it so I could see. Her black jumper had slipped a bit off her shoulder and I could see her green bra strap. Suddenly, it was hard to focus on the phone.

"I film Anu's bullying when I can," she told me. For evidence. I even filmed her bullying you."

Freya came closer, and I could smell her vanilla perfume. She leaned on my arm and I froze. My heart was beating way too fast.

"Here," she said.

I watched Anu's last attack on me. It was weird, like a film in which I was the main character.

"If Anu knows we've got evidence," Freya said, "she'll stop."

I didn't care about Anu right then. I was too busy staring at Freya. She was saying "we" again, like there was a "we". Like there was an *us* ...

"Cal?" Freya asked. "You OK?"

She was so close that her breath felt hot against my cheek.

"Er, yeah," I said. "Er, catch you later ..."

I didn't even wait for her to reply. I just ran down the corridor and hid in the toilets until I'd calmed down.

*

As I left school that day, I found Jacob sitting on the steps by the main door.

"Hey," I said, with my best friendly smile. "Did you like *Year One?*"

"Was OK," Jacob said. "The drawings were cool. And the fighting."

"I've got more at home."

"Yeah, you said." Jacob grinned. "You live in a library?"

"No." I shrugged. "Just thought you might want to see them."

"Maybe," he said, and he stood up. "Gotta go, geek. Smell ya later ..."

I watched him leave. Maybe we might be friends, after all? I smiled, but not for long.

"Oi – dork!"

It was Anu.

But just before she reached me, Freya appeared.

"Leave him alone," she said.

"Who's this – your girlfriend?" Anu asked. "Is this *Geek Love Island* or summat?"

"Yeah, it is actually," Freya said. "Leave Cal alone."

Anu looked like she might hit Freya. But then we heard another shout.

"Freya! Come on ..."

It was her mum. Freya looked at me. "You're coming, too," she said.

"Me?"

"Yes you, Cal!" she said. "Or would you rather stay here?"

I shook my head and followed her.

"Geeks in love," I heard Anu say. "I wanna puke …"

It was nice to get a lift and all the way home I didn't think about Anu or Jacob. All I could think about was Freya. Something felt odd – but in a really, really brilliant way.

"See you tomorrow, Cal," Freya said, when we got to my house.

"Er, yeah," I said. "That'd be cool."

"Maybe you should give me your number?" Freya said with a smile. "We could talk about our mission …"

She dropped her voice to a whisper so her mum wouldn't hear.

"*To get Anu …*"

"Only one problem," I told her. "I don't have a phone."

Freya grinned. "OK, geek boy," she said. "See you in class, then."

6

Young Justice

Two days later, we were at the food bank when I saw Jacob's mum come in and start chatting with my mum. Jacob pulled a face and went back outside.

Martin could see that I was nervous. "What's up, kid?" he asked.

"That angry lad," I said. "I want to talk to him."

"So why don't you?"

"I don't know how to without upsetting him," I said.

Martin smiled and I spotted his crooked teeth again.

"Sometimes you have to confront hard stuff," he told me. "It's the only way."

"OK," I said. I still wasn't convinced, but I took a deep breath and went outside.

Jacob was sitting on the low wall of the church car park.

"Hey ..." I said.

He spun round, shocked. "What you doin' here?" he asked.

I felt nervous and silly, and a bit scared. Jacob was a lot tougher than me.

"I help out sometimes," I said.

"Help out?"

I nodded.

"I saw you last week," I admitted.

"S'pose you think I'm a scumbag, then?" he said in a low voice.

"No," I said. "Why would I think that?"

Jacob scratched his left cheek but he didn't look at me. I saw that his nose and ears were pink with cold.

"Cos I'm one of them scroungers," he said, and he looked kind of sad. "Me and me mum. Bet you had a right good laugh."

"No way," I told him. "I just come here with my mum. She wants to give something back."

Jacob looked up at me. "What, like help the poor and all that?"

"Kind of," I said.

"So, you're like those other rich kids at school? Thought so ..."

"Not really," I told him. "We're not rich. Not like Anu and –"

"She's a cow," Jacob said. "A right bitch. You should hear what she calls me."

"But she's wrong," I pointed out. "You don't *have* to listen to her. You're not a bad person."

"You sound like the teachers," Jacob said as he stood up. "I don't care if I'm a bad person. Everything's bad in my world."

I didn't know what to say, so I stayed silent.

"Have you told anyone about seeing me here?" Jacob asked.

"No." I shook my head. "I wouldn't do that."

"Make sure you don't, either," Jacob said, and the menace was back in his voice.

"I won't," I told him. "I don't want trouble. I thought we could be friends ..."

Jacob laughed in my face.

"I don't need no one," he said. "Friends let you down. I'm better off on my own – *thanks*."

I was about to reply when Jacob's mum came out.

"Come on, love," she said. "It's cold out here."

Jacob took her arm and I saw that he towered over her.

"Remember," he hissed at me. "Don't even think about telling anyone."

*

After dinner, in the park across from my house, I thought how Jacob was wrong – everyone needs friends. Life without friends is rubbish. Not that

I *had* any close friends. Maybe I wasn't all that different to him really ...

"Hello, day-dreamer," a voice said. It was Freya on her bike, with her curly hair all messy. "Fancy doing something?" she asked.

"Like what?" I said. I felt all hot and cold at the same time, and my legs had gone wobbly.

"You could invite me to your house?" Freya said. "Come on. I can even show you where you live."

Mum broke into a huge grin when we walked in.

"Freya!" she said. "How lovely to see you!"

"Hi, Mrs Gill-Smith," Freya said. "I bumped into Cal and he asked me over. Is that OK?"

As they chatted, I wondered what I was supposed to do. Should I get Freya a drink, maybe something to eat? Should we stay in the kitchen, or go into the living room? What if she wanted to see my bedroom?

We ended up in the living room. Freya sat on the sofa, with me on the armchair. She'd taken off her shoes and sat with her legs crossed, holding a glass of apple juice.

"So, why did you come round?" I asked, a bit confused.

"I wanted to see you." Freya shrugged. "For help with my mission to stop Anu. Plus, I felt bad for you."

"So you're here because you feel sorry for me?" I asked.

"No," Freya said. "I like you, too. I've liked you since nursery. But that was different, obvs ..."

"Huh?" I said. What did she mean by "*like*"?

"I like you," she repeated. "You're smart and funny – and strange. I adore strange people."

"But ..." I began.

"Look," she said. "You're not making this very easy."

She put her drink down and stood up. Her eyes were wide under her glasses, her nose was red and her hair was messier than ever.

"Well …" she began, as she sat on the arm of my chair.

I felt nervous and sick and excited all at once. Was Freya about to ask me out? Was she about to become my first girlfriend?

"I'm a geek, and you're a geek, and I think we should, you know, hang out together," she said.

"*Hang out?*" My voice went all high-pitched with disappointment.

"Yes," Freya said. "Like, be friends and do stuff together."

"Oh …"

"Well?" she said.

"Yes," I said at last. "Yes, totally …"

Freya smiled. "I thought you might say that," she said. "Now, are you going to show me your Batman collection or what?"

7

Young Avengers

Freya decided that our first trip out would be to the cinema. She called it a "play date", which was a bit weird and embarrassing, but I was happy just to be with her.

That weekend, we got tickets for the film of a book I'd read at school. We had no choice – there were no comic book films on, and no fantasies either.

"It's probably rubbish," Freya said. "But I'm not watching Pixar with the five-year-olds."

We were standing in the line for snacks and I hadn't got a clue what to talk about. "I don't mind what we watch," was the best I could come up with.

"I should take off my hat," Freya said. I guess she was struggling for small talk too.

She stuffed her red woolly hat in her coat pocket. I thought she looked really pretty in it, but I didn't know how to tell her that.

I had on my favourite Batman T-shirt, for good luck. I'd even changed my socks. I didn't tell her that, either.

"So, favourite superhero ...?" Freya said.

"Batman," I said. "He's the best ever."

Freya raised an eyebrow.

"But he hasn't got any super powers," she said.

"Yeah, and that's why he's the best," I said. "He's more human than the others and he's got a dark side, too. Who's your favourite?"

"Jessica Jones."

"But she's Marvel ..."

"Yep!" Freya said, as she grabbed a pick 'n' mix bag. "She's super strong, super clever, and she doesn't take any rubbish from boys. She's kick ass."

"I'm more into D.C.," I told her.

"One million quid says Jessica Jones would kick Batman's ass." She looked at me and smiled, and her eyes were all sparkly.

"Never!" I said. "Batman wouldn't fight her anyway – cos she's a girl."

"But Batman's too cool to be sexist," Freya argued.

Was that true? I'd never thought about it.

"So if I kicked you," Freya went on, "would you kick me back?"

"No."

"What if I punched you?"

"I don't fight," I said. "Fighting makes things worse."

"That explains Anu Patel," Freya said with a nod. "It's why you don't stand up to her, isn't it?"

"Yeah," I said. "And she's tougher than me."

"But the harder they come, the harder they fall," she half-sang.

"Huh?"

"It's from an old song my mum loves," Freya said. "You need your own Jessica Jones. To save you from Anu."

I grinned at her.

"Is that you?" I asked. "With your super strength?"

"Nope," Freya said, and her eyes looked even more sparkly. "With my super intelligence, wit and charm. Oh, and my phone."

*

I was right – the film was rubbish, and Freya complained all the way home in her mum's car.

"Boring, stupid, silly nonsense," she moaned. "Nothing happened. Like, nothing at all. She was all into the boy, and the boy didn't care and her parents were getting divorced and *blah, blah, blah!*"

Freya's mum dropped me off and Freya waved as they left. I grinned back, but as I started to cross the road, I saw Jacob. He was trudging into the park, head down.

"*Jacob!*" I shouted, but he didn't hear me.

I ran to catch him up, but when I did, he looked embarrassed.

"Get lost!" he said, and he rubbed his face with his sleeve like he'd been crying.

"What's wrong?" I asked.

But he swore and stormed off.

"Jacob!" I called, and I ran after him. "I just want to help ..."

This time, he stood there, blubbing, with his nose all snotty.

"It's shit!" he wailed. "It's all total shit!"

"What is?" I asked. "Has someone hurt you?"

"Forget it," he raged. "It's nothing to do with you."

He was right, but I couldn't just ignore him.

"I want to help," I said, but it came out all wrong. Like I was begging.

Jacob looked right into my eyes. "Why?" he asked. "You've been on my case since I started at your school. Why?"

I shrugged. "I just ..."

"See?" Jacob said. "You don't really care –"

"I wanted to help you settle in," I said.

"But you don't even *know* me," Jacob said. "I'm just some new kid, innit? Been in five different schools since Year 5 –"

"Why?" I asked. "Why do you keep moving schools?"

"Stuff," he said, and he shook his head again. "You wouldn't understand."

I looked over the road to my house.

"Come on," I said, and I did my best to sound forceful. "It's freezing out here. Come back to mine."

I waited for him to say no – to swear and walk away. But he didn't. Instead he wiped his tears on his sleeve, sniffed up a load of snot, and nodded.

*

Jacob stayed until just after nine. We sat in my room at first and looked at comics and books. Then I showed him my dad's studio in the shed, which he said was really cool. He walked round the rest of the house like it was a castle or something and Mum fussed over him. She made him soup and cheese on toast, then two mugs of tea and a slice of cake. When his mum came to pick him up, Jacob looked kind of sad to leave.

"Sorry, Jas," his mum said to mine. "He gets like this sometimes ..."

"It's no bother," my mum said with a smile. "Jacob is welcome any time."

"See you tomorrow?" I said to Jacob. "In school?"

"Yeah." Jacob nodded. "Why not?"

I didn't know whether to shake his hand, bump fists or nod back at him. In the end I did none of them. I just smiled.

8
Dead End

Next morning, Jacob smiled when he saw me.

"All right?" he asked as he sat down.

But then he leaned in close and whispered. "Don't say anything about yesterday, *yeah?*"

I nodded. "I wouldn't," I said. "I'm not like that."

When Freya arrived, she was surprised to see Jacob next to me.

"You're in my seat, you know?" she said.

"*Yeah?*" Jacob said. "Who are *you* – his girlfriend?"

Freya went a bit red. Behind us, I heard Anu Patel snigger with her friends.

"It's like car crash TV in here," I heard her say. "May I present – *The Abnormals!*"

Jacob turned and glared at Anu.

"*Problem?*" he asked.

Anu blushed, but it shut her up. Then Jacob looked at Freya.

"So, you want this seat?" he said.

Freya grinned.

"After the way you shut Anu up?" she said. "You're more than welcome!"

They smiled at each other, and I felt a stab of jealousy. What if Jacob liked Freya too? What if she fancied him?

"But Cal's mine first," Freya added.

I squirmed, but it felt great to hear her say that.

"No worries," Jacob said. "He ain't really my type ..."

*

The three of us had the same lessons all morning, so we hung out together. It felt strange – I'd never had any proper friends at school before. But I wasn't complaining. And nor were the teachers – Jacob's good mood shocked them. He was cracking jokes and smiling, and doing his work at the same time.

"I don't know what you had for breakfast, Jacob," Miss Spargo told him. "But I *like* it ..."

At lunch, we found three seats together.

"I've got cheese, pickle and mayo with salad," Freya said.

"I've got soggy bolognese wraps that Dad made," I said. "Plus an apple, a banana and a cherry yoghurt."

Jacob looked over at the hot food counter.

"Better get mine," he said and he got up and wandered over, as Freya opened her lunch.

"Bit weird," she said, mid-bite.

Most people who talk while eating annoy me, but not Freya. If anything, she looked even cuter.

"What is?" I asked.

"You and Jacob," she said.

I told her what had happened, but I left out the crying bit. Freya nodded and took another bite.

"He's quite nice," she said. "But I knew he would be."

"Yeah," I said. "He seems much more chilled ..."

"Anu got a proper shock, too!" Freya said, and her eyes sparkled with delight.

I smiled back at her, but it fast turned into a frown. Over her shoulder I saw Myles Granger heading for Jacob, with his gang in tow.

"*Oi, chav!*" Myles shouted.

Jacob turned to face Myles.

"What you up to?" Myles asked, squaring his broad shoulders and pushing his floppy blond hair off his face. I knew loads of girls fancied him, but I didn't understand why. He was a bully – always smirking, always nasty.

When Jacob didn't reply, Myles sneered. "Lost your tongue?"

I watched as Jacob clenched and unclenched his fists.

"Scrounging tosser!" one of Myles's gang snarled.

"That's right, innit?" Myles said. "You're one of them dirty benefit rats."

Myles went right up to Jacob and shoved him hard.

"Get lost!" Jacob yelled.

And then he turned and ran.

I made the mistake of watching him, which meant I caught Myles's eye.

"Yeah, geek?" he said. "Missing yer boyfriend?"

He laughed, then left with his crew. I felt hot with anger, and my appetite was gone.

"I'm going to check on Jacob," I told Freya.

"OK," she said with a sigh. "But not without me …"

*

We found Jacob sitting on a fire escape behind the English department.

"Leave me alone," he muttered.

"Myles Granger is an idiot," Freya told him. "Just tell the teachers what he did."

"I'm no grass," Jacob said.

"Who cares about that?" I asked.

"I said leave me alone." Jacob stood up. "I'm fine."

Freya took her lunch from her bag.

"I've eaten a bit," she said, "but you have the rest."

"Me too," I said. "I'm not hungry …"

Jacob looked at Freya's half-eaten cheese sandwich. "You got any bad germs?"

Freya grinned. "No more than you."

"Come on," I said. "Let's get back to class."

Jacob took Freya's sandwich and wolfed it down.

"Nah," he said, as he took my lunch leftovers too. "I don't fancy it. I'm off home."

I wanted to stop him, but he would have ignored me. He stuffed my wrap and fruit into his pockets. Then he walked across the grass, climbed the fence and jumped down onto the road behind school.

"He'll get into trouble," I said.

"He's always in trouble," Freya said. "Something tells me he isn't bothered."

Jacob's good mood hadn't even lasted a whole school day. I wondered what he would tell the teachers tomorrow. But in the end, it didn't matter. Jacob took the rest of the week off. And then he turned up at my house, out of the blue.

9

Geek Squad – Assemble!

Mum sat in silence, as Jacob's mum explained. It was early Saturday morning and I was still in my pyjamas.

"There's no one else I can ask," Jacob's mum said.

"It's fine, Janice," Mum told her. "No bother at all."

"I'm really sorry," Janice said. "I don't want to impose ..."

Mum shook her head. "Really," she said. "It's no trouble."

Jacob was sitting at the kitchen table. His mum needed to visit her brother in hospital, so she had asked if Jacob could stay at ours that weekend.

I could tell Mum was surprised, but she didn't seem annoyed.

"Jacob never makes proper friends," Janice was saying. "And he really likes Cal ..."

I was a bit embarrassed, but Jacob smiled at me and so I smiled back.

"Of course he can stay," Mum said. "We'd love to have him."

"Oh, thank you!" Janice said. "I'll be back by tomorrow evening. I'm so grateful to you all, Jas."

Mum and Janice got up and walked into the hall.

"You hungry?" I asked Jacob.

"Yeah," he said.

"Toast and cereal?" I offered.

"You can tell me the truth," Jacob said.

"About what?"

I grabbed some butter and jam from the fridge.

"Like, if you don't want me here," he said. "I don't mind –"

"I don't mind either," I told him. "It'll be fun."

"Hello," Dad said as he walked into the kitchen. "I hear you're staying with us this weekend, Jacob?"

"Yes," said Jacob.

"Great!" Dad said. "I've got some things you can help with."

"Dad!" I hissed.

"Ah! It's only a few bits," Dad said. "You don't mind, do you, Jacob?"

Jacob grinned. "No, Mr ... er ..."

"Just call me Dominic," Dad said.

I stuck four slices of bread into the toaster, then asked Jacob what cereal he wanted.

"Dunno," he said. "You got Frosties?"

"Nah," I said. "Healthy options only – bran flakes, granola or Weetabix."

"Whatever," Jacob said with another grin.

After two bowls of Weetabix and three slices of toast each, I had a shower and got dressed. Jacob sat and looked at a pile of comics in my room.

"So what shall we do now?" I asked.

"Dunno," he said. "Whatever."

For the next hour, each time I offered Jacob any sort of choice, he replied with "dunno". In the end, I took him down to Dad's studio.

"Ah," he said. "Are you two ready to give me a hand?"

Dad was taking apart his old workbench. As he undid the bolts and screws, I helped Jacob take the wooden panels outside and pile them up. But Jacob seemed more interested in my tent. It was dumped in a corner, all crumpled up.

"Never been in a tent," Jacob said.

"What?" Dad asked from under the remains of his old bench. "*Never?*"

"Nope. My Gramps always promised to take me camping, but then he …"

Jacob didn't finish.

"You could camp tonight," Dad said. "In the garden."

"But, Dad," I said, "it's December."

Dad slid out from under the bench. His glasses were wonky and he was covered in sawdust.

"So what?" he said. "Where's your sense of adventure, Cal? If you make a campfire, you'll be nice and toasty."

I looked at Jacob.

"Dunno ..." he said. "Whatever."

"OK, then!" I said. "It'll be a laugh."

The tent was torn in places and the frame was bent too, battered by the wind during a Lake District holiday the year before.

"We need to patch it up," Dad said. "Jacob – pass me that penknife, please."

In the end, it took Dad and Jacob two hours to fix the tent, and I spent most of that time watching them. I saw how Jacob paid close attention to everything Dad did. He even helped to sew up the ripped fabric. When they were done, they both looked really proud.

"Put the kettle on!" Dad told me. "We're parched. Biscuits too, please."

As I filled the kettle, the doorbell rang.

"Cal – it's Freya!" Mum called.

Oh no. I had completely forgotten that she was coming over.

"Hey!" Freya said from the kitchen door. "Ready for our play date, Cal?"

Then she spotted Jacob.

"*Oh.*"

"Hi," Jacob said. "Cal never said you were coming –"

"He probably forgot," Freya said with a glance at me. "It's no big deal. What are you two up to – anything fun?"

Dad came in and told her how they'd fixed the tent.

"Jacob's mum had to go away," I added. "So he's staying over and we're camping tonight."

"Cool!" Freya said. "Room for one more?"

*

Mum spent ages on the phone with Freya's mum, making sure it was OK for Freya to camp with us. When at last she was done, she gave us all a stern look.

"We are trusting you," she said. "Trusting you to behave, to be respectful –"

"Mum!" I moaned.

"Quiet, Cal," said Mum. "This is important. Freya and Jacob are my responsibility in this house."

"We know," I told her.

Mum nodded, and then she took Freya home to get her toothbrush and stuff. Jacob waited until they were gone.

"Ha ha!" he said. "Tonight's gonna be *well* funny."

"Why?" I said.

Jacob punched me on the arm. It was supposed to be playful, but his fist felt like a hammer.

"*Ow!*"

"Sorry!" he said. "I didn't mean to –"

"No worries," I told him, rubbing my arm. "What do you mean *funny*?"

"You and Freya," he said.

"What about me and Freya?"

"Mate, anyone can see you fancy her."

"But I –"

"It's obvious, Cal!" Jacob said. "And she fancies you, too. I'm gonna be stuck in the middle – in a flipping tent!"

"But we're just friends," I protested.

"Yeah, right!" Jacob said, and he gave me a nudge that sent me sprawling. "Shit – sorry!" he said, but he was laughing too much to pick me up.

"Just shut up about Freya," I told him. "And *stop* shoving me around – you're like a baby elephant!"

Jacob grinned.

"Mate, you're weird," he said. "You're proper on another planet."

10

Geek Squad – Rise Up!

Dad helped us put up the tent, and then we threaded big pink and white marshmallows onto wooden skewers. The fire was already going in a metal grate Mum had placed on some old slabs. Every now and then Jacob and Freya added more wood. We ate hot dogs with ketchup and mustard for tea, and it was fun, despite the cold.

As darkness fell, the only light came from the fire, and it smelled amazing. When we added the marshmallows, it got even better. We were sitting on cushions, on top of old blankets, and we had hoodies and jackets to keep us warm.

"Do you think there are any ghosts round here?" Freya asked.

"Don't believe in ghosts," I told her.

Jacob shook his head.

"You can't say they *don't* exist," he said.

"I can," I said. "Where's the proof?"

"Every culture in the world tells ghost stories," he insisted. "They can't all be making them up."

"Yeah," said Freya. "What if they're, like, all around us? Floating about between worlds that we can't see?"

I felt a shiver run down my back.

"That'd be proper cool," Jacob said. "Like that old film where the boy could see ghosts!"

"*Sixth Sense*!" Freya said. "My parents *love* that film."

Jacob took his marshmallows from the fire and blew on them.

"*I see dead people ...*" he whispered, and Freya shrieked.

"But seriously," I went on. "No way are ghosts real."

Just then Mum came out with bowls of treacle sponge pudding with custard.

"Thanks, Mrs G-S!" Freya and Jacob chanted.

"Yeah, thanks, Mum!" I said. "This is awesome!"

Later on we sat around chatting and then I made hot chocolate and found some more marshmallows. When I got back, Freya was talking to Jacob.

"Why do you get so angry?" she said. "Like, at school?"

Jacob shrugged.

"You don't have to tell us," I said.

"I don't mind," he said. "It's just hard to talk about, that's all. I kind of keep stuff to myself ..."

Freya was sitting really close, and the flames lit up her face. As I sat down, she touched my hand and smiled at me.

"I've never had a dad and Mum went away when I was born," Jacob said at last. "She couldn't look after me. I didn't meet her until I was eight ..."

"Oh, Jacob," Freya said. "I'm *really* sorry. I didn't mean to be nosy."

"S'OK," he told her. "Mum was taking drugs and stuff, and my grandparents brought me up until she got better."

"And then you moved away to live with her?" I asked. I remembered how he'd said he was always the new kid.

"Not like that," Jacob said. "My Nan got cancer. I was seven when she … er … went."

Freya put her hand on his arm.

"You don't have to tell us any more," she said. "We get it."

Jacob smiled.

"Might as well tell you now I've started," he said. "After Nan died, my Gramps found life really hard. He always *pretended* to be happy, but I knew he was sad. When I was in bed, he used to sit downstairs and get drunk and cry. I spied on him sometimes. But I never hugged him or said anything."

He rubbed his eyes, and Freya squeezed my hand again. She looked like she might cry too.

"I thought he might get angry," Jacob went on, and he turned to look at me. "If I saw him crying …"

"I cry," I told him. "And I don't care who sees me."

"Yeah, but my Gramps always told me men don't cry," Jacob said. "He was an Army boxer. And then, when I seen him cry, I …"

Jacob stopped and stared into the flames. Neither Freya nor I spoke.

"Then Mum came back," Jacob said. "We started being a proper family. But Gramps got sadder. One day, he took me down by the old railway and the river. It was his secret place. He said I was all Mum had and I had to grow up."

Jacob looked into the fire for a long time. I watched his marshmallows melt in the flames.

"Gramps promised to take me camping," Jacob went on. He was crying properly now. "But it never happened. He just left one day …"

"Oh, Jacob," Freya said. "Look how upset you are. I'm so sorry."

"It's OK," he said. "The police found Gramps's body at the river. He was holding a picture of my Nan."

He sat up and looked at us. "Since then, me and Mum just move around – most times it's because I get excluded. Sometimes, I go down to the river and talk to Gramps. I've built this den …"

"That's cool," Freya said.

Jacob nodded.

"Used cardboard and plastic sheets and bits of wood," he said, almost proud now. "Gramps would love it."

"Does your mum know?" I asked.

"No one does," Jacob said. "You have to promise not to tell anyone."

"You can trust us," Freya said.

"You have to make a pact," he told us. "Like blood brothers and that."

He spat into his palm.

"Go on," he told us. "Do the same."

"*Euurghhh!*" Freya said. "I'm not doing that."

"Freya ..." I said, and I spat into my palm.

She sighed and copied us. As we all shook hands, she pretended to puke.

"Gross," she told us. "Why can't you have nice, clean rituals instead of these silly macho ones?"

"We're connected now," Jacob told us. "Blood brothers."

"*Ahem*," Freya said.

"OK." Jacob smiled. "Sisters, too!"

*

We sat up until 2 a.m., talking and telling stories. When at last we got into our sleeping bags, I was still thinking about what Jacob had said. I lay staring into the darkness. What a weird day.

Like Jacob, I'd never really had any close friends. Now, all of a sudden, I had two. My life felt like it had changed. It felt different, but great too. Like things were all shiny and bright.

But that feeling didn't last very long.

11

The Dark Knight Falls

Just two days later, the shiny brightness wore right off. One minute I was eating my lunchtime sandwich, the next Jacob rushed me. His eyes bulged with fury as he grabbed my school jumper. I had no idea what was happening, but it felt like I was being manhandled by a gorilla.

"It was you!" Jacob screamed. "You must have told them!"

"W-w-what?" I said.

"You lying little shit!" he yelled, and he clenched his free hand into a fist.

Mr Ahmed and Ms Jenkins rushed in before he could punch me. He was swearing like mad as they dragged him away.

"Think you've upset chav boy," Anu Patel sneered. "He thinks you told everyone."

"Told them what?" I asked, my stomach churning with fear.

"About scrounging at a food bank ..."

My heart sank. *I* hadn't told anyone.

"Hate to be you when Jacob comes back from exclusion," Anu added.

I grabbed my stuff and stormed to the library where Mrs Collier was sitting behind her desk. Her kind face creased with concern.

"What's happened, Cal?" she asked.

"Jacob went for me," I told her. "He thinks I told everyone his secret."

"What secret?" she asked.

I shrugged and dumped my bag on the floor.

"Doesn't matter now."

I sat in a corner, and pulled a random book from the shelves. But I couldn't focus because I was so wound up. Then Freya found me.

"Have you heard?" she asked.

"Yes," I told her. "Jacob *attacked* me in the hall."

"But it was Myles Granger – not you!" Freya said.

"Huh?" I said. "How do you know?"

"Because I heard him tell everyone," Freya replied. "But why didn't you tell *me*?"

"Jacob made me promise," I told her. "I couldn't break his trust."

"Fair enough," she said. "So what now?"

"We find Jacob," I said. "Come on, let's go."

The exclusion room was in the admin corridor, and out of bounds to pupils without permission. But for once I didn't care if I got into trouble. Jacob needed to know the truth.

"Are you sure?" Freya said.

"Yeah, course. He's our friend and we have to help him."

The admin corridor was deserted, but we waited a moment, just in case. When no teachers appeared, I opened the door and whispered.

"Jacob ..."

He was sitting on a chair with his head in his hands. He didn't look up, so I tried again and Freya joined in.

"Hey!"

This time he did hear. He frowned when he saw us.

"It wasn't me!" I whispered.

"Yeah right."

"He's telling the truth," Freya said.

Jacob stood up and I couldn't help but feel scared. After the way he'd been in the dinner hall, I didn't know what to expect. But I saw that his face was more sad than angry now.

"It wasn't me," I said. "Honest."

"It was Myles," Freya said. "He told everyone."

"Get lost!" Jacob snapped. "Like Myles would know!"

"Freya *heard* him," I said. "Myles's dad owns a restaurant by St Margaret's. He saw you."

Jacob didn't say anything.

"Why would I tell anyone?" I asked him. "We made a pact, remember?"

"We're telling the truth," Freya said. "I promise."

Jacob thought about it. "Myles?" he said.

"Yes," Freya insisted. "You know he hates you."

Jacob nodded.

"I'm sorry I grabbed you," he told me. "I wasn't thinking. I was just –"

"We have to stop Myles," Freya said, and I remembered something she'd told me.

"Yeah," I added. "He might be tough, but the harder they come ..."

"The harder they fall!" Freya finished. She beamed a smile at me.

Jacob's face grew stony.

"You're right," he told me. "We have to bring Myles down."

I heard the doors open behind us.

"*Calloway! Freya!*"

Ms Jenkins didn't sound too happy. We turned and trudged towards her.

"What are you doing here?" she asked us. "Do you have permission?"

"We're just trying to help Jacob, Miss," I replied.

Ms Jenkins' face softened.

"Come on, Cal," she said with a half-smile. "I know you mean well, but you must obey the rules."

"But Jacob didn't do anything!" I protested. "It's that Myles Granger, he's nothing but a bully and a trouble-maker."

"Leave that to me and Mr Ahmed," Ms Jenkins said. "Neither you nor Freya should be here without permission."

"But you can't punish *him*!" Freya insisted.

Ms Jenkins sighed and led us away.

*

Jacob stayed in isolation, and Anu and the others were nasty about him all afternoon. It was hard to ignore them and for the first time ever I wished school would end early. Not even Mr Ross could keep my attention and I love History.

I rushed out with Freya when the lesson ended. But, in the main corridor, we knew something was wrong. The word "Fight!" hung in the air and people were pushing and shoving to get out of school fast.

"I've got an awful feeling that it's Jacob in trouble," I said to Freya.

"Me too. Come on, run!"

We ran out to find Myles by the school gates, with two other Year 10 lads. They were holding Jacob tight by the arms, and they were laughing at him as he struggled.

"STOP IT!" I shouted without thinking.

"Stop it! Stop it!" some older kids mocked.

I didn't care. I dropped my bag and ran over. I didn't know what I was going to do. But I had to do something.

"Leave him alone!" I said, and I tried to pull Jacob away.

"Piss off," Myles's mates jeered.

"Get lost, you little shit!" Myles warned, as he punched Jacob full on the mouth.

Jacob struggled but Myles's two henchmen were too strong even for him.

"Get a teacher!" I heard Freya scream.

"You dirty little scrounger!" Myles yelled. "Think you can have me?"

My heart was racing and I was almost sick with fright, but I had to help Jacob. I grabbed Myles and tried to push him away.

"Stop!" I shouted. "Leave him alone!"

But Myles just shoved me to the ground and I heard laughter ripple in the crowd. Then someone shouted "TEACHERS!"

I saw hand after hand holding phones in the air, recording everything. Jacob was struggling and shouting, like he was in a kind of blind rage.

"Please!" I begged as I jumped to my feet. "Just let him go."

Myles grinned at me.

"I warned you," he said.

I saw his fist flying through the air. I heard Freya scream my name. I heard gasps from the crowd. All in a split second ...

Myles's fist caught me hard under my chin. I felt my head snap back and my body start to fall.

And then my world went black.

12

Batman Forever

I woke up in hospital, with a nurse staring at me.

"Hello!" he said. "Welcome back."

"Cal!" I heard my mum's voice say.

She appeared from my right, and started kissing and hugging me.

"Mum ...!"

"I thought you were seriously hurt," she sobbed. "I didn't know what to do."

"Give the boy some space, Jas," I heard Dad say.

His face appeared from my left with a too-bright grin.

"Hey!" he said. "Sore?"

I smiled and tried to nod, but my whole head throbbed.

"Owww!" I croaked. "Why am I here?"

"You had a nasty fall," the nurse told me in a soothing Caribbean accent. "You banged your head on the ground."

"I don't remember that," I said. "I just saw Myles's fist and then –"

"SSSHHH!" Mum said. "Forget about that. Just get some rest."

"Where's Freya?"

"She's here – she went to get a drink." Mum smiled.

My head hurt, my jaw hurt, my legs felt like jelly. I tried to sit up, but I sank back down again, dizzy.

"Was Jacob OK?" I asked.

"Everything's fine," Mum said, with a look over to Dad. "Just rest."

I gave her a glare, but Mum refused to say any more. She and Dad went to get some coffee.

"You need an X-ray," the nurse said. "Just to be safe. It was a nasty fall. Now, hush, and let me get that sorted for you."

*

They let me go just after 9 p.m., but I was still groggy.

"Where's Jacob?" I asked Freya.

"He beat Myles up," she said. "Then the police came and arrested him."

"*Why?*" I was shocked. "Myles started it ..."

The rest of the trip home passed in silence. At Freya's house, she gave me a peck on the cheek.

"I'll see you after school tomorrow," she said.

At home, I couldn't sleep. I was sore and I was angry. Myles had picked on Jacob, then punched me. So why was Jacob in trouble? When I asked Mum, she shrugged.

"That's the law," she said. "Apparently Jacob went berserk."

"Have you spoken to his mum?" I asked.

"No," she said. "Janice won't answer her phone."

And so I lay awake until 3 a.m., fretting about Jacob.

*

"It's freezing out there," Freya told me when she came over the next day. She took off her woolly hat and blew on her hands. "How's Batman?"

"I'm fine," I said.

"Apart from the bruises and the sore head?"

"Never mind that," I said. "What happened with Jacob and Myles?"

"It's all rumours," Freya explained. "But Jacob's been excluded. Mr Gossage told us –"

"We need to see him," I said.

Mum appeared at the living room door.

"I've spoken to Janice," she told us. "Jacob is fine, but the school won't have him back."

"This is all so wrong," Freya said. "Horrible and wrong."

"Perhaps," Mum said, "but that's not the point. Jacob has ... *issues*."

"No!" I snapped, so loud I shocked Mum and Freya, and myself too. "Jacob doesn't have *issues*. It was Myles! Look what he did to me."

"Cal," Mum soothed, "I know you're looking out for your friend, but it's up to the school – there's nothing you can do."

I knew she was right. I knew it, but I hated it. After she'd gone, Freya sat down beside me.

"Are you OK?" I asked.

"Yeah," she said. "I'm here with my best friend. What could possibly be wrong?"

I smiled.

"Is that what I am?"

"Yes," Freya said. "And maybe something else, too."

I gulped, all nervous again. Did she mean ...?

"You're Batman," she said. "The way you took on those lads. You were really brave."

"Oh – that," I said.

"Cal!" Freya insisted. "You stood up for Jacob. You tried to save him. Never mind superhero powers and all that rubbish. You're a *real* hero."

"But ..."

She leaned over and kissed me. It was so sudden, and so fast, that I didn't have time to react. Her lips were soft and I could taste strawberries. It was lovely – as if she'd just eaten some sweets.

"But ..."

"Oh Cal, shh," she said. "Say nothing."

*

I was in a much better mood that night. I took my painkillers, read a comic and fell asleep thinking about Freya and that strawberry kiss. I felt older somehow, more like a proper teenager. It was like I'd stopped being a geeky kid. I'm sure I fell asleep with a great big smile on my face.

But then the house phone rang, and woke me up right in the middle of a dream. It was 4.03 a.m.

13

Nightrunner

Jacob had run away.

"I heard him banging about," Janice said. "But I just thought he was in a strop."

"When did you realise he was missing?" Mum asked.

"I woke up around 2 a.m.," said Janice. "I went into the kitchen for a glass of water and I found his note on the table."

Mum nodded. It was now 6 a.m., and I couldn't stop yawning. The kitchen was cold and flecks of snow were falling outside. Janice's hands shook as she held her tea, and there were dark bags under her eyes.

"I didn't know what to do," she said. "I mean, I called the police but –"

"You were right to come here," Mum said. "You shouldn't be alone."

"He's done it before," Janice said. "But this time feels different. He was so upset yesterday – the worst I've ever seen him. He's had such a hard time, what with his grandparents and my troubles ..."

Mum nodded, and told Janice that she understood. Then she looked at me. "Cal, are you well enough for school?" she asked.

"I'm fine," I told her. "But I want to stay here. The police might find Jacob."

"No," Mum said. "Sitting around won't help. I'd rather you went back today."

*

Freya gave me a huge smile when I got to school.

"*Yay!*" she said, but then we both shut up as Mr Gossage walked into class.

"Ah, Cal," he said. "Great to see you! Could you and Freya stay behind please?"

I sat down, wondering what Mr Gossage wanted. Behind me, Anu Patel was sneering as usual.

"*Great* to see you, Geek Boy," she said. "You back, then?"

I turned to face her. Something inside me had changed and, for the first time, she didn't scare me, not one bit.

"Yes," I said. "And I'm sure you're thrilled ..."

"*Ooh*," she said. "Snarky *and* brave after your little beating."

Before, I would have cowered, but not today.

"I'm bored of you." I turned to face her. "Bored of your stupid games and your bullying. Please stop it."

"Ha ha!" she mocked. "Geek Boy fights back. And there was me thinking we had an understanding."

"Not any more." I shook my head. "You can do your own homework from now on."

"I don't think so," Anu said. "Since when did you tell me what to do –"

"Oh, shut up!" Freya snapped. "You're such an idiot!"

"*Anu!*" said Mr Gossage. "*Enough!*"

"But, sir, I ..."

"I said *enough!*"

When everyone had gone, Mr Gossage came and sat by us in the empty classroom.

"I need you to tell me what's going on," he said. "I know what Myles did that day, but is there more?"

"More *what*, sir?" Freya asked.

"*Bullying*," Mr Gossage said. "Miss Spargo and Mrs Collier are particularly concerned and both have named Anu Patel. We've also had incidents posted on social media –"

I looked at Freya. Neither of us did social media, so we hadn't seen anything.

"Anu bullies Cal," Freya blurted. "I've got *evidence.*"

"She's just –" I began, but Mr Gossage held up his hand.

"Hang on, Cal," he said. "What evidence, Freya?"

Freya showed him the videos she'd recorded on her phone and we both watched Mr Gossage's face grow darker as each incident played out.

"There's more," Freya told him. "Anu forces Cal to do homework and projects, and she sells his work to other pupils –"

"*What?*" Mr Gossage said. "Is that true, Cal?"

I nodded, too embarrassed to speak.

"Right!" Mr Gossage said. "Don't look so worried, Cal – but both of you get to your lessons now. I need to speak to Mr Ahmed and Ms Jenkins about this."

On our way to Science, I managed at last to tell Freya about Jacob.

"What do you *mean* he's missing?"

"He ran away," I explained. "Last night. His mum is at my house and the police are looking for him."

"Oh, no," Freya said. "Poor, poor Jacob."

*

Jacob was still missing when Freya and I got home. Things weren't looking good. Mum had called a doctor for Janice, who was asleep in our spare bedroom.

"The doctor gave her something," Mum said. "To help her sleep. I'm dealing with the police for her –"

"What have they said?" Freya asked.

"Nothing, really," Mum said. "They might do an appeal for information on tonight's local news."

"On the telly?" I asked.

"Er, yes. Where else?" Mum said. "They need to find him. He's young and vulnerable. Plus, the forecast is for snow. Imagine if he's on the streets somewhere."

That was when I realised. I had been *so* stupid. I looked at Freya and moved my eyes up to the ceiling.

"What?" she said.

"*Books.*"

"What books?" she asked, confused.

"The ones we need for the project about *rivers.*"

"Pardon?"

"Badgers build dens by *rivers*, remember?"

At last, her eyes lit up.

"Oh," she fibbed. "For *that* project ..."

We dashed up to my room, and I shut the door.

"Of course!" Freya said, and she jumped up and down.

"SSSH!" I told her.

"How dim are we?" Freya said. "He's gone to his secret den. We should tell your parents!"

I shook my head. I knew I was taking a huge risk.

"Look," I said. "We promised Jacob we'd never tell."

"Yes," Freya said, "but this is *serious*. It's not some silly game where we spit into our hands."

"Jacob feels like he's been betrayed all his life," I replied. "If we break our pact, he'll never forgive us!"

"But he's missing –"

"No," I said. "Not if we know where he is. We'll find him and bring him back."

"But we don't know where his hideout is," Freya said. Her eyes were big and shocked.

"We can *find* it," I told her. "Come on! Are you with me?"

Freya thought for a moment.

"OK," she said. "Batman and Jessica Jones to the rescue. I'll have to tag along, just to keep you out of trouble."

A plan formed in my head – a massive gamble. If it worked, we'd all be fine. If it didn't, Freya and I would be in *big* trouble. But I didn't care about trouble right now. Jacob needed us, and we'd made a pact.

All that mattered was saving Jacob before he fell too hard.

14

Club of Heroes

When we told Mum we were going to the cinema, she thought it was a great idea.

"It'll take your mind off things," she said.

"Yeah," I said. I felt sick with guilt. I'd never lied to Mum on purpose before. "We're going to the multi-screen in town."

We stopped by Freya's so she could change into warmer clothes and dump her school bag. Fifteen minutes later, we were outside the cinema.

"So," Freya said. "Care to explain the secret mission?"

I nodded.

"We need your phone. Have you got it?"

Freya grinned.

"Of course," she said. "*Oddball*."

We opened Freya's Maps app and found where we were. Then we zoomed out to see the whole city. But every time we made the map bigger, the street names disappeared. It was hopeless.

"Library," I said. "We need a proper map."

"*Now?*"

"Yes – now," I said. "The reference library's open till seven."

Within ten minutes, we were hunched over a big paper map. I traced my finger around it, until I found the railway station.

"Jacob told us the den is where the railway line and river meet," I said. "So we start here and follow the line."

"Ooh," Freya said. "You've engaged Detective Mode."

"Huh?" I said.

"From the Batman video games?"

"Never played them," I said.

"*Never!*" Freya said. "You can't be a Bat-Geek and not play *Arkham*! Holy cow!"

"Ssh!" I whispered. "It's a library, remember."

I followed the railway line towards the river, but at no point did they meet.

"What do we do now?" I asked. "Jacob definitely said river and railway, didn't he?"

Freya thought for moment.

"Move over, Bats," she said.

This time she followed the line. But where the river and railway were closest, she stopped and moved left.

"Jacob said *disused* line," she said. "And if you look here, there's an old bridge over the river. I reckon this is where he meant."

She tapped the map and grinned.

"Wow," I said. "That's real Detective Mode."

An old railway map showed that Freya was right. The line had been scrapped in 1987. Next we found bus timetables.

"Number 16," Freya said. "It's not far. We get off on Meadway Avenue, where it meets Stonebridge Road."

As we walked across town to the 16 bus stop, I felt like I was the star of my own comic. I had my favourite girl with me, and a friend to rescue. All that was missing was a cape.

*

Stonebridge Road was a deserted dead end that stopped at the river. Above us, the disused line sat on a steep bank protected by a tall fence. The bridge itself was grimy and covered in graffiti. It was freezing cold, and the one working street-lamp buzzed on and off.

"It's spooky here," Freya said. "What if we get mugged?"

"Who's going to mug us?" I asked her. "There's no one around."

We scanned the area for signs of Jacob. But the fence was solid and topped with barbs. There was no way Jacob had climbed it.

"Look!" Freya said. She grabbed my arm. "See where the road ends. There's a wall and some bushes. We could go that way."

She was right. A thick wall cut the road off from the river. But between the wall and the end of the barbed fence, was a tiny gap. Freya crouched and shoved her way through the tangle of bushes. I followed and when I stood up, she pulled a torch from her pocket.

"Bet you didn't bring one – *Bat Boy*!" she said. "Jessica Jones – practical *and* cute."

We trod carefully along the old river path, towards the bridge. The mossy stone was wet and slippery, and it would be a big problem if we fell into the cold dark river. We went under the bridge, past random heaps of boxes, a rotten mattress and an upside-down shopping trolley. Somewhere in the gloom, we could hear a *squeak squeak squeak*.

"Yuck!" I whispered. "Rats!"

As we came out on the other side, I heard a scramble to my right. Freya shone her torch towards the sound and gasped.

"I bloody knew it!" a voice said.

Jacob stepped out of the bushes and stood in front of us. His face and clothes were thick with grime.

"I knew the Geek Squad would show up," he said with a lopsided grin.

*

Five minutes later, we were sitting on the bank with Freya squashed up between Jacob and me.

"The police took me in," Jacob said. "They said Myles and his mates could press charges. I didn't know what to do and so I came here."

"Your mum's mad with worry," I told him. "She's round at ours."

Jacob shook his head.

"I can't go back," he said. "The coppers will charge me, and school has already kicked me out. I beat them up really badly. Myles wasn't moving when I ran off."

"We'll help," Freya said. "We spat into our palms, remember?"

"Did you tell them?" Jacob asked. "About this place?"

"No." I shook my head. "Like Freya said, we made a promise. But the police are looking for you."

"What's the point in going back?" Jacob said. "I'll just start another school, get into trouble, be a big fat problem for everyone."

"You don't *have* to get into trouble," Freya said.

"Yeah," I said. "You can decide *not* to fight …"

Jacob shrugged.

"To be honest," he said. "You two are my only real friends."

Freya reached over and kissed Jacob on the cheek.

"We'll always be friends," she said. "But you'll freeze to death if you stay here."

Jacob looked away, towards the river.

"Sometimes I think that would be the best thing," he said. "Like Gramps …"

"*No!*" I said. "No way! You're coming back with us. Otherwise the bad guys win!"

"But why?" Jacob said, and I could hear the despair in his voice.

"Because your mum loves you," I said. "Because you're a good person. You've got a whole future ahead of you. You can be anything you want. You just have to start with happy!"

I was breathless and sweaty, and I realised my fists were clenched tight. I didn't even sound like me. I sounded like my mum. Freya was looking at me with her mouth open in surprise.

"No one can bring your Gramps back," I went on. "Or change what's happened in your life. But it's still your life, isn't it? It's still something you can change and make better."

Jacob grinned.

"Are you gonna beat me up if I don't?" he asked.

"No," Freya said. "He won't. But I will."

"Well, I don't hit girls, so ..." Jacob said.

"That's sexist," Freya said. "But I'll let you off, just this one time."

Jacob led us to his den. It was just a plastic sheet, tied to some tall bushes. He'd made soggy cardboard walls, propped up with bricks and sticks. He'd laid out more cardboard for a bed, and had three cans of baked beans in a row. But he left all that behind. All that mattered was a framed photo.

"Come on, Gramps," I heard him whisper. "Let's go before Cal gets really mad and gives us double detention and makes another speech ..."

I was about to nudge him for mocking me when I saw a bag tucked under the cardboard.

"Don't forget these!" I said. I grabbed the bag – it was full of graphic novels.

Jacob took Freya's hand, then mine, and the three of us walked back under the bridge as snow fell thick and fast.

"You know what?" Jacob asked.

"What?" Freya and I said together.

"You two are pretty sound – for a pair of geeks."

"The name is *Jones*," Freya said. "Jessica Jones ..."

A few weeks later

I got to pick the film, but Freya insisted on buying the tickets herself.

"Did you see what happened to Anu?" she asked as we stood in line for popcorn.

"Yeah," I said. "I felt sorry for her."

"Cal!" Freya said. "You can't save everyone."

Mr Ahmed had acted fast. Anu was excluded, and her best friend Maddie moved schools. Anu's dad arrived to take her home just as the bell rang. It felt like the whole school was there to witness it, and I couldn't help cringing. It must have felt so humiliating for her.

Anu had kept her head down, as her dad told her again and again how stupid she was and how she was an embarrassment to her family. I was one of the few pupils who didn't laugh. I stood and watched, and at last I understood why Anu was such a bully. She'd had a good teacher.

"Sweet or salty?" Freya asked. She pointed at the popcorn.

"You decide," I told her. "You always do, anyway."

Myles Granger was permanently excluded too, along with two of his gang. No one missed them – they were the meanest bullies in school. After they left, life got a lot easier for everyone.

"Sweet, please," Freya said, just like she always did.

"I wish Jacob was here too," I said.

"What are the chances of that?" Freya said with a shrug, and then she sauntered off to get pick 'n' mix.

We'd tried to win Jacob a reprieve, but it didn't work. Mr Ahmed still kicked him out. But Jacob was lucky in other ways. The police decided not press charges, especially after so many pupils told on Myles and his gang.

We'd all promised to stay in touch, but Christmas had come and gone, and we hadn't seen him. We'd done a few shifts at the food bank and Mum had called Janice a few times, but they were always busy. Jacob had moved on, and it bothered me. He was a real friend and I missed him.

"Some idiot just stood on my foot," I heard Freya say.

"Huh?"

"Over by the foam bananas," she said. "I need my Batman."

I didn't know what she expected me to do, but I followed her to the pick 'n' mix.

"*Awright*, Batman," a voice said.

"Jacob!"

He looked different. His hair was longer, and he seemed relaxed, almost happy. Freya nudged me and started giggling.

"Did you two set me up?" I asked.

"Yeah!" they said together.

"We made a pact, remember?" Jacob said. "Just cos I'm at a new school, it doesn't mean I've forgotten my geek squad. Not after what you did for me."

"We'd better get another ticket," I said.

"No need," Freya said. "I bought three. Me in the middle, and my two best mates either side. Come on!"

I looked at Jacob.

"You OK?" I asked. "Like, *really* ...?"

"Yeah," he said. "Now come on, Bats – your girlfriend's waiting."

About *The Harder They Fall*

Over the past few years, I have grown more and more troubled and angry at the rise in poverty in the UK. From our towns and cities, to the countryside and the coast, more and more people are being forced to make ends meet with less.

The UK is one of the richest countries on Earth, yet every day children go to school hungry, those with disabilities struggle to pay bills, and pensioners and parents go without. The Trussell Trust, which runs 400 food banks in the UK, gave out over 1.1 MILLION food parcels between April 2015 and March 2016, and the situation is getting worse rather than better.

On the other hand, people from bankers to politicians, from footballers to so-called celebrities, are getting richer and richer. In the meantime, the poorest people in society grow ever poorer as they fall even further behind the richest. The Office for National Statistics, which is the UK's official voice on these matters, says that the situation is unbalanced in the extreme.

For example, 10% of households in the UK own 45% of the UK's wealth. By way of contrast, the poorest 50% of households own only 8.76% of the wealth. You can read more facts like these on the Equality Trust website.

So, when I was thinking of this story, I knew that Jacob and his mother would be poor. I knew they would be among the millions of people in the UK who go hungry every day for different reasons, from benefit delays to an unexpected bill while on a low income. They would need to use one of the many food banks that provide emergency food and support to people in crisis.

Far too many people think that poverty is about people not working or about them being "lazy". It seems to me that our society has lost its empathy for poor people partly because of TV shows like *Benefits Britain*, and constant negative news stories.

But the truth is that poor people aren't just numbers. And they aren't just stereotypes either, to be picked on or shouted at. In writing about Jacob and his mum, I wanted them to be characters that showed the human face of poverty. Real, everyday people who have almost nothing and who struggle to survive. I also wanted Jacob to be one of those lads who everyone thinks is a "lost cause". I refuse to believe that any child is past saving. And I cannot stand the massive gap between the richest and the poorest. I think it is unjust and immoral.

Of course, Jacob's life isn't easy. But that doesn't mean that he – or you – should give up. There are no easy answers and no shortcuts to happiness – although great friends can make life feel much better. It's true that sometimes hope can seem lost, but it is always there, however hard it might be to find.

But *The Harder They Fall* is more than a story about food banks, poverty and "lost causes". More than anything, it's about friendship and hope, and looking after the people you care about. I wanted this story to be funny and interesting and exciting. And I wanted it to make you, my readers, think about the society in which we live. I hope you enjoy reading it as much I enjoyed writing it.

Warmest wishes
Bali Rai

When life feels really hard

Jacob in *The Harder They Fall* is vulnerable to feeling suicidal. His grandfather killed himself, and now he feels so intensely negative about his own life that he cannot see the point in carrying on. Jacob is able to talk with his friends about how he feels, but mental illness is something many people find very difficult to talk about.

If you are struggling with how you feel and need to talk, you can call these free helplines. They offer comfort, advice and protection to children and young people.

Childline (UK)
0800 1111

Samaritans (UK)
116 123

Our books are tested
for children and young people by
children and young people.

Thanks to everyone who consulted on
a manuscript for their time and effort in
helping us to make our books better
for our readers.